To Anna.

The Light And The Dark

By
Dennis Gibbons

Dennis Gibbons
(Sharon's brother)

THE LIGHT AND THE DARK

Published by
Words & Phrases
2231 South 14th Street
LaCrosse, Wisconsin 54601

copyright 1998 by Dennis Gibbons
All rights reserved

ISBN:1-57502-695-3

January 1998
First Edition

Printed in the U.S.A. by:
Morris Publishing 3212 E. Hwy 30
Kearney, NE 68847

Odi et amo- "I love and I hate"
    Catullus, A Roman lyric poet

Introduction

Good and Evil. Ying and Yang. Light and Dark. Life is many things including conflict-man against nature, man against society, man against woman, woman against man, men and women fighting themselves. Without conflict, we don't have a story.

Once again, I've concentrated on the theme of love. More has probably been written on this subject than anything else. We may never fully understand it, but we do know love has many faces including happy, sad, and angry. We also know that we all have the capacity to make someone so happy or hurt them so much. Most of us have probably been swept up in love's joys and sorrows.

We love and we hate. We forgive, we get even, laugh, cry, and go through a number of other emotions. We will always search for love, it makes us human.

I've tried to balance out my poetry, but it appears the sadder side to love dominates. Just as Medieval or Renaissance painters could always depict hell better than heaven, the artist of today still produces more dark than light. Can we identify more with pain or does conflict bring out more universal feelings? You be the judge.

Dennis Gibbons
LaCrosse, Wisconsin
1997

Table of Contents

Introduction By Author

Section I - Love, Life and Reflections?

Love Is Not 3
There Lives 4
We Filled A void 5
Three Wishes 6
What Are You? 8
I'd Rather be 9
If You Ever 11
Sometimes, we 12
Games 13
The Solution 14
Toxic People 15
That Mystery Girl 16
You're Not Alone 17
That Kid 18
Horses 19
Not A funny Tale 20
Black Ice 22
The Little Girl And The Snake 23

Section II - Alcohol and the Night

I Do The Same 27
Paths 28
The Light and the Dark 30
The Woman Sitting there 31
Into The night 33
The Race 34
Make A choice 35
Colors 36
Searching 37

Hitler Built The Autobahn	*38*
The Drinking Calendar	*39*
Football Seasons Come At last	*41*
Blue Smoke	*42*
Why Do I draw Them?	*44*
Sinking Ships	*45*
The Beacon	*46*

III. Forgiveness

I Could Never Hate You	*49*
Why You Are That Way	*51*
I Never Thanked You	*52*

IV. The Pain of Love

I Think we could Have Made It	*56*
It Would Have Been so Simple	*57*
I Celebrate	*58*
The Things I Never Gave You	*59*
Faded Pictures	*60*
I Wanted It all	*62*
Enter Through The Doorway	*64*
Flew To Me	*66*
First Loss	*67*
The Last Regret	*69*
The Sea Shell	*70*
What Ever Happened?	*71*

V. The Lighter Side

When Will I leave You	*75*
Some Have A puppy	*76*
Snuck up on me	*78*
The Mid-life Blues	*79*
Sweeter Than	*80*

Where have They Gone? 81
Should Have Seen 82
Didn't Make My Day 83
Love Is Like Candy 84

VI. The Bitterness of Love

Have I Ever Thanked You? 87
Eve of Destruction 88
The Showdown 89
Threw Me for A loss 90
Should I compare thee? 91
We Can Be Friends 92
You Annoy Me 93

VII. Love and Beauty

When You Had That glow 96
Grandma Rocking 97
The Changing Sea 98
What Do You See? 99
Drifts 101
Flowers In The night 103
What Is their Secret? 104

INDEX OF FIRST LINES 106

VIII. Return To The Diner 109

About The Author - a candid interview 131

I. Love, Life and Reflections

*"A find, a fire, a heaven, a hell,
where pleasure, pain, and sad repetance dwell."*

-Richard Barnfield

"A season pass on the shuttle between heaven and hell."

-Donald Dicerman

Love Is Not

Love is not a faucet
Turn it off at will
A mess we simply clean up
When we let our feelings spill

Love can get away from us
When we don't use our brain
Emotions drive us recklessly
Like a runaway freight train

"Humans aren't logical"
A famous Vulcan said
Feelings overtake us
When we don't use our head

Love is not perfect
Never meant to be
Love is commitment
Not running free

Love is not judging
Making someone what they're not
Love is accepting
And forgiving a lot

Love is not a faucet
Emotions sometimes flow
Love is being there for you
No matter where you go

There Lives

You stand there so smugly
Doing anything you can
Handle any women
Manipulate any man

You are so carefree
Nothing bothers you
The life of every party
Making everyone a fool

Those drawn to you
You bait with casual tease
Acting so innocent
As you brush them off with ease

No one can get too close
You've made sure of that
Those who try soon regret
The sting of your attack

Defense mechanisms shrewdly built
You've constructed such a maze
Trying to break through it
Would put Freud into a daze

Behind those gray walls
Beneath the castle keep
Down psychic steps of fear
Where truthful feelings sleep

Into the darkest dungeon
Where shadows bend and twirl
Imprisoned in a chamber
Lives a frightened little girl

We Filled A Void Together

We filled a void together
Although years apart
Leaving special memories
Etched into each heart

You must have been so flattered
A doting older man
Wishing so much to see you
He risked everything at hand

There were no commitments
You felt safe with me
Someone who would love you
But let you still be free

And I was able to absorb
Your youthful energy
Time no longer mattered
I could deny mortality

One night it finally happened
As I gazed into your eyes
A painful truth swept over me
But I had to realize

You became the daughter
That I wanted so
And I replaced the father
That left you long ago

Three Wishes

Found an old dusty lamp
Polished it bright
A geni popped out
"A wish for you tonight"

"I want the girl I love
To feel the way I do
She must adore me
Her feelings deep and true"

"Secondly, I must request
A much better job
Enough to support us both
Without working like a slob"

The geni shook his head
Smiled and raised his voice
"I can't do all of that
What's your second choice?"

"Seeing her now
Gives me lots of stress
Feelings tear me up inside
Make my life a mess"

"If you can't make her
My wife or lover
Let her be my friend
Like a sister and a brother"

"Friendship takes a lot of work
Its built on faith and trust
I can't make you two be friends
By tossing up some dust"

"If I can't have her as a friend
And she won't be my wife
My final wish is simple
Erase her from my life"

"I have to deny that request
I wouldn't even dare
You'd hate yourself forever
Giving up the one for who you care"

"Let this be your wish
Tell her that you care
And if she ever needs you
Be sure to be right there"

"You seem like such a nice guy
She must be quite a girl"
He waved and spun and dissapeared
In a inky, smokey swirl

I reflected on his words
What message did he send
We can't make someone love us
Or force them to be a friend

What Are You

What are you afraid of?
It can't be based on fear
Love is something deep inside
Nurtured and sincere

Is it that you can't forget
Some lone and distant lover
Who wrenched your heart so bad
That you never did recover?

Or do you look at others
And feel thankful to be free
Broken marriages, shattered dreams
Those caught in love's debris

Or do you feel the need
To chase the world around?
Never stopping to catch a breath
Or firmly touch the ground?

You let your guard down for awhile
An open door with light
Then slam it so quickly
That it echoes in the night

You're safe in that cocoon
Constructed through the years
Safe, but so alone
Trapped within your fears

"I'd Rather Be"

I'd rather be lonely
Why chase the world around?
Looking for relationships
That never end up sound

Stable but boring
Will kill you really slow
But exciting and unstable
Will quickly take a toll

I learned a painful lesson
My last love being you
Never let my guard down
No longer play the fool

Staying busy as I can
With my work and play
Hide my feelings in the night
Shield them through the day

Put on my "happy face"
Party with them all
Joke, dance, and drink
But you won't see me fall

Walk away from late night glitter
Leave behind the music clatter
Push through the crowds
Say,"goodbye," to mindless chatter

Tolerating sleepless nights
Returning to the womb
Safe, but all alone
Inside my empty room

Carefully draw the covers back
"The last turn of the screw"
Nestle with my pillow
Pretend that I'm with you

If You Ever

If you ever ask me
To please stay away
I'll respect your wishes
And sadly walk away

Its not your problem
If you let me go
But I know you don't want to hurt
The one who loves you so

But if you ever want
To enjoy a gorgeous day
Or hold my hand and whisper
In a dimly-lit cafe

Or if you ever need
To talk or get away
I'll be there for you
And chase the blues away

When storm clouds gather
If you can't hold on for the ride
Just write or call
And I'll rush to your side

If you ever untangle
The web inside of you
And finally realize
You feel the way I do

If you ever want someone
Whose love is always true
Just say the word and I'll be there
To spend my life with you

Sometimes We Have To

Sometimes we have to use our head
Not listen to our heart
Boldly face reality
Even if it tears us apart

"The Bard" was right
Fate does not lie in a star
We often make the life we lead
Determine who we are

Decisions made or not
Things beyond our control
Facts we can't deny
The fact I love you so

You have tried your best
Overcome a lot
Accepted what you are
Denied what you're not

The situation is awkward
The problem which we deal
You can't help who you are
I can't help how I feel

Although I miss you so
Think of you night and day
It makes it harshly simple
To choose to stay away

Games

Games of the mind
Games of the heart
Games pull us together
Games push us apart

Vulnerable walls go down
Escape the lonely hell
Hurt claws deep inside
Return into the shell

Broken whispers
Silent prayers
Painful gazes
Bitter stares

A hollow laugh
A phony tear
A convenient lie
A hidden fear

Shakespeare knew it well
Life's a play at best
Actors put on a mask
Put others to the test

The Solution

The solution may sound crazy
I might appear a fool
Finally solved the problem
Of loving both of you

You're both so beautiful
Independent and so strong
But she's the one I want to marry
Please don't get me wrong

Love you both, you understand
But she may not survive
Needs me more than you
Her life's on such a dive

The remedy that I propose
Might seen a little wild
But I know I want her to be
The mother of my child

We'd all be so happy
I know it would be true
You would be a god-mother
My daughter named after you

Toxic People

Beware of toxic people
You'll find them all around
They're unhappy with their lives
Seek to bring you down

You may see them at work
Or observe them where you play
They want to stir the pot
So wisely walk away

Beware of toxic people
What can their motive be?
Projections of their failures
Or just green-eyed envy?

Poison you with gossip
Disarm you with lies
Set you up to fall
Down before you realize

Walk away from such people
Who so easily condemn
They're bitter with self-pity
Try not to be like them

That Mystery Girl

Do you know that woman?
The one men want to know
Writes into magazines
Appears on some talk show

Claims she wants someone sensitive
A man who'll treat her well
Doesn't want someone harsh
Or some co-dependent hell

She likes to go to dinner
Enjoys a slow dance
Doesn't need to slam shots
Until she's in a trance

Really wants romance
Candles in the dark
Intelligent conversation
Walking in the park

I've met her phony copies
Who tell you all those lies
Say, "Can't find someone nice"
Then search for lousey guys

If she really does exist
Where can this woman be?
If you know her where-abouts
Send her straight to me

You're Not Alone

Has life dealt you cruelly?
Feel your dreams shattered?
Love has wronged you?
Left your heart tattered?

Think you're the only one
Whose faced such strife?
People and fate conspired
Chose to wreck your life?

When it comes to pain
No one is a stranger
You're not the only one
Don't feel like the Lone Ranger

Life is hard at times
So complain or cry or pray
Then pick up the broken pieces
Tomorrow is another day

Don't drown in self-pity
Dwell on those who have done you wrong
Do the best with what you have
And you should get along

That Kid

Met you in high school
Noticed something unique
Beyond the dimples
And radiant smile

Saw you years later
Flattered you remembered
Still had those dimples
Disarmed me with a smile

Cute kid to pretty woman
Drawing men
Like a streetlight
Draws mayflies

But your uniqueness
Has little to do with beauty
You're strong and independent
Spiritual without being religious

When tragedy struck
I prayed you would survive
You rode out the storm
Stood tall-didn't lose that smile

Now, when I see you
Admire your strength and beauty
I still say to myself
"I like that kid"

Horses

I love horses
Their beauty
Their grace
Lovely symmetry

There are many breeds of horses
Short and tall
Thin and heavy
Some neigh too much

Horses can be unpredictable
A mild mare
Can turn into a bronco
Throw you hard

The last few horses
Were like that
A peaceful canter
Became a ride to hell

Grasp the reigns
Let up on stirrups
Nothing works
Fly out of the saddle

Broken, bruised, a muddy pasture
Find myself thinking
"I love horses"
"But won't ride one for awhile"

Not A Funny Tale

There was a pretty young maid
Sparkling eyes-skin so fair
A messmerizing smile
Locks of pretty hair

Her parents drank too much
Her father ran away
She never knew stability
Only careless play

A restless spirit drove her
She couldn't settle down
So she found exciting work
In the tavern in the town

There was an old prince
He went out for a ride
Had his heart broke many times
But still searched for a bride

He met her at the tavern
It was love at first sight
But he was old, she was young
And it didn't seem just right

But he gave her gifts
Wrote poems-couldn't stay away
She loved him too, but toyed with him
Feared he wouldn't stay

They both were so afraid
To trust anyone with their heart
So it appeared inevitable
That they soon would part

But the game went on for years
She never did slow down
The prince finally gave up
And rode out of the town

It's not a funny tale
In fact, it's rather sad
I'm not sure of the details
But know it ended bad

The maiden lost her youth
Young men turned away
She escaped into a bottle
Just to make it through the day

The old prince just got older
Ended all alone
If he's still alive
He's in a nursing home

The moral to the story
Cuts right to the bone
Don't take a chance with love
Die bitter and alone

Black Ice

The highway of love
A smooth ride often
An occasional bump
But usually worth the ride

Suddenly, it happens
You don't see it
But you feel it
Panic strikes!

If you use your brakes
You'll slide
Don't use them
Smash up anyway

Wheels of the brain swerve
Tires of the heart burn
You slide and swerve
Crash-a wrecked relationship

The highway of love
Can be treacherous
So beware of
Black ice

The Little Girl And The Snake

Have you heard the fable
The little girl and the snake?
How she should have known better
But made a big mistake?

The little girl was playing
In a grove of trees
Suddenly, saw a snake
Coiled up by her knees

The snake looked quite harmless
Even pretty in a way
But she should have known the truth
And wisely walked away

"Little girl, please pick me up"
She heard the serpent say
"We can be such good friends
Play games throughout the day"

"I know what you are!"
She answered with a cry
"You're poisonous and will bite me
And I will surely die!"

He stuck out his forked tongue
Caught the young girl's stare
"Promise I won't hurt you
Promise I'll be fair"

She picked up the snake
He coiled around her tight
Exposed his lethal fangs
She felt his fatal bite

The little girl let out a scream
"Why did you have to lie?"
"I trusted you, you let me down
And now, I'm sure to die"

The serpent finally told the truth
"I am what I am and you are you
You knew what I was
I'm evil, but you're a fool'

Saw you just the other night
Wouldn't make that mistake
Tempted first, but soon remembered
The little girl and the snake

II. Alcohol and the Night

Drinking- *"The happiness that it brings is merely negative, a momentary cessation of unhappiness."*

-Bertrand Russell

Night- *"When the shadow of death is darkest, when despondency is strongest, and when hope is weakest."*

-Charles Dickens

I Do The Same

I do the same as I did then
That painful day long ago
Standing by so helpless
When life dealt me that blow

I do the same as I did then
As I slowly watch you die
I try and fail and try again
But you'll never see me cry

My male ego won't let me
You know that macho pride
Where we try to act so tough
And hide our feelings deep inside

I'll be there if you want me
I'll even say a prayer
I'll hold you when you need it
And forgive you if I dare

You won't draw me into it
With your fatal kiss
But I will fight to pull you back
From the alcohol abyss

I feel a tightness in my throat
My eyes are soon on fire
Watching you slip and slide
And drown in that quagmire

I do the same as I did then
At my grandpa's funeral, I stayed calm
And blocked the well of tears
And dug my fingers into my palm

"Paths"

The path you chose to take
Was not a path at all
Nothing but a muddy track
Leading to your fall

Perhaps, you had no choice
Growing in that gloom
Too late to make a change
Too willing to face the doom

I could have taken you
From that dreadful life
Making you happy
You could have been my wife

Giving all I had
A family and a home
Making you feel needed
Instead of all alone

The ones who claimed to love you
Helped choose your path to hell
And I, the one who loved you most
Couldn't catch you if you fell

So, you don your jeans
Gulp a beer
Hate the face
Inside the mirror

Slam another drink
Hop into your car
Hit the accelerator
Head toward that bar

Greet your peers
Catch your breath
Join your "friends"
On the path to death

The Light and the Dark

The lighter side of you
I know and understand
The laughing eyes-that smile
The tender touch of hand

But the painful moment comes
Drawn to the dim-lit candles of your eyes
A shiver rushes over me
As I see your darkside rise

The smoothness of your voice
Is reduced to senseless muttering
The eloquent walk is now a stagger
Your eyelids are fluttering

When you hurt yourself like that
I am hurting too
Why must you do this to us?
Why must you make me Blue?

When the dark triumphs for awhile
It kills the one that I adore
When you crawl into a bottle
I don't know you anymore

The Woman Sitting There

The dream became a nightmare
I raced ten years ahead
A painful bolt shook me
Woke up and felt the dread

There was something famaliar
The woman sitting there
Bleary eyes soon caught my gaze
Through matted strands of hair

Not like the girl I love
Who has shiny, healthy hair
Eyes that sparkle when she laughs
So unlike the woman sitting there

Lines are drawn on the face
Of the woman sitting there
Sleepless nights and alcohol
Revealed in her despair

The girl I love has vibrant skin
But partys way too hard
Fears commitment like a plague
And won't let down her guard

The woman sitting there
Was never someone's wife
Never had children
Or straightned out her life

She's forty looking fifty
Her ship of hope has sunk
She can only play pathetic games
With another hapless drunk

She must have thought she knew me
Looked up from her beer
A painful recognition
A shed of silent tear

Into The Night

Blues music blares
Lava lamps bubble
Behind the bar
Patrons guzzle

Greet you as you enter
Knows your name
Knows what you drink
Even knows your game

Drinks in every word
Makes you feel at home
Shows concern for you
So you don't feel alone

Dimples in her cheeks
Lights up with a smile
You soon forget your problems
Feel good for awhile

Races around the bar
Catching every glance
Cheerfully refills drinks
With an agile prance

Finally says goodbye
Makes you feel alright
Feel a rush of warmth
As you step into the night

The Race

With a cheetah's speed you race
Then continue your attack
Toward terminal velocity
Never daring to look back

You plunge into your work
To escape who you are
Then race to meet plastic friends
Who hang out at some bar

You carefully don the bogus mask
Then enter with a smile
Alone in a crowd's the worst
But you can pretend for awhile

Don't stop to smell the roses
Why try to ease the pain?
Work and play until you drop
Or else you'll go insane

Partying is for the young
Work's not everything
Burning candles will catch up to you
Self-destruction is what you'll bring

Why continue with the frantic race?
It'll kill you can't you see?
Are you afraid to stop and look around?
Because you're lonely just like me?

Make A Choice

Maybe it sounds funny
Isn't it just a scream?
But why do we go on
If we abandon every dream

You might think me weird
I must be a fool
Want more than get you in my bed
Get stinking drunk with you

Doesn't it sound funny?
Why do I even bother
To say, I'd think I'd make
A good husband and a father

Time is running out
I can't wait too long
Hope you pick the proper path
Not the one that's wrong

You can stay with that crowd
The one's who like to use you
Think they're such good friends
When they continue to abuse you

Continue where you're going
Stay on that slide
Drinking, chasing, always racing
A subconscious suicide

Or you can choose the other path
Which one will it be?
Nowhere in a hurry?
Or take a chance with me?

Colors

If you don't watch out
You're really going to fall
Keep up what you're doing
End up against a wall

Colors will gang up on you
Are you to blind to see?
A rainbow of death surrounds you
But you still race carelessly

Blackouts will get worse
You can't win that fight
Your face will turn a rosey-red
Your liver will turn white

Your fingers will turn yellow
Your eyes a bleary brown
Your outlook will turn blue
As you waunder all around

You still have time, but must be strong
To block that fatal fall
Before "colors" overtake you
And your killed by alcohol

Searching

Searching for your inner-self
Find out who you are
Think you'll really find the truth
Living in a bar

I would never interfere
I'm not on a "savior kick"
But when I see you hurt yourself
I feel myself get sick

Pour yourself a drink and slam
Crawl out from the bar
Watch a so-called friend of yours
Pour you into a car

Get up in the morning
Ashamed of what you've done
Reflect a little through the day
Was it really that much fun?

The daytime headache dissappears
You feel your really sane
The sky gets dark, the stars come out
You do it all again

Hitler Built The Autobahn

Hitler built the autobahn
Smoking calms you down
A hog can find an acorn
Somewhere on the ground

Some people win at gambling
I know two or three
But know so many others
That don't lose gracefully

Some people live a long life
Stuff themselves with every treat
And someone who eats rice cakes
Gets killed jogging down the street

Some people drive drunk every night
What can their secret be?
If you or I pulled such a stunt
We'd get caught immediately

Some people are fun to be around
When they've had a drink or two
Hitler built the autobahn
Drinking can be cool

There's an exception
To just about any rule
Look at the exception
Live life like a fool

A Drinking Calendar

The New Year has come at last
Bring on all the cheer
Forget the resolutions
Drink a lot of beer

February is for lovers
Don't forget your Valentine
Candy and flowers won't do it
Give her lots of wine

You don't have to be Irish
End late winter depression
Be a happy drunk
Without all the oppression

If Good Friday falls in April
Tell the boss you cannot work
Sneak off to happy hour
Behave just like a jerk

Mermorial Day in May
Forget those who have fought and died
Pack your picnic cooler
Go out and get real fried

Summer has finally come
Enjoy each day in June
Forget sports and nature
Get drunker than a loon

America has its birthday
Fireworks exploding near and far
Watch and shout, "Hooray"
Then head straight for a bar

August has few holidays
It's usually hot and dry
Cool yourself off with booze
Watch the summer fly

September brings the school year
Put those textbooks down
Head right for a house party
Bring the rafters down

October can be depressing
Except for Halloween
Be a real-life monster
Get drunk and then get mean

Thanksgiving with the family
The best excuse of all
Say things to hurt each other
When you've had too much alcohol

Christmas is a joyous time
Get your yuletime worth
Stay hammered through the holidays
Forget the peace on earth

Football Season Has Come At last

Football season has come at last
Break out the brats, stock up on beer
Buy yourself a pennant
Get ready to whoop and cheer

Put on your favorite jersey
Argue which team is best
Watch those modern gladiators
Put each other to the test

Brave young men push down the field
You gasp at every pass
Hope the receiver connects
Doesn't fall in the grass

Sometimes you get so angry
Shout at the TV screen
"The "ref" was blind, he was inbound
Your favorite coach gets mean

Isn't it enough to enjoy
Each play of every game?
Do we have to be fanatics?
Do we have to act insane?

But it gives us a chance
To escape life for awhile
Soon forget our problems
Even force a smile

Football season has come at last
It is time to lose our head
Consume a lot of alcohol
Bet on each point spread

Blue Smoke

Catch your gaze
Through swirling blue smoke
You smile-toss your hair
Part the drunken sea

"Want to dance?"
You nod-pull me close
Feel soft feminity
Burn against me

Taste the perfume
On your neck
Hear your heart
Feel your breath

Exchange life stories
Make each other laugh
Over frosted mugs
Dance only the slow ones

Reality strikes
Lights go on
"Drink up people!"
"Walk you to your car?"

"I don't know you," you reply
"And I don't know you"
The Nineties-we mistrust
Ourselves and each other

Squeeze my hand fiercely
Reluctantly break the bond
"I'll call," I whisper
Taste the sweetness of your mouth

You push the perfumed paper
Into my hand, I turn
You smile back
Red eyes in blue smoke

Weeks pass, then months
Snow against the windows
Unfold the crumpled paper
Still catch your scent

Close my eyes
Mind floods back
Gold memory in blue smoke
Wonder why I never called

Why Do I Draw Them?

Why do I draw them?
Do they want me to save them?
I know most people want to be rescued
Only when their backs are to the wall

Do they want to
Drown me with them?
A funeral pyre
Doused with alcohol?

Do they view me
An understanding father-figure
A stable force
In their turbulent world?

Am I an over-grown boyscout?
Or do I fill a selfish need
Finding meaning in
Their loss?

Has my life become a country song
Love in all the wrong places?
But the poisoned fruit
Appears at nearly every social function

Why do I draw them?
We all get something
Out of a relationship
I drink, but not like them

Sinking Ships

There's an old sea story
Rats desert sinking ships
Don't know if its true
But true friends desert sinking drunks

They haven't stopped caring
Its that they care so much
No longer can bear the pain
Watching someone they love self-destruct

I watch you weigh anchor
Raise the sails
Fear a fateful voyage
Pray you survive the tempest

Wicked clouds approach
Wind rises
Torrents of rain
Slashing sea

There's another sea story
Ships scream before breaking up
Will you shriek out
Then dissappear beneath the waves?

I stand helpless on the shore
It's all up to you
Hope you can steer around the rocks and shoals
Return to port safe and sober

The Beacon

You're strong and proud
Nothing wrong with that
But like a character in a Greek tragedy
You have a fatal flaw

When you step into the night
Think of me
No matter where you go
My spirit will be there

I too have a fatal flaw
Shouldn't play God or social worker
Judge others
Should only be your steadfast friend

If the fingers of doom descend
Catch you offguard
Blind you like a Minnesota blizzard
Making you lost and frightend

Think of me as a beacon
You have to help yourself
But I can provide the light
To guide you out of the storm

III. Forgiving

Forgiveness- *"The fragrance the violet sheds on the heel that has crushed it."*
-Mark Twain

I Could Never Hate You

I could never hate you
No matter how hard I try
I could never hate you
My heart can never lie

The touch of your hand
The way you looked at me
The dreams I hoped to live
Were never meant to be

You promised nothing
I read too much in you
I thought you were the one
But too good to be true

I clung on to the fantasy
Hoping you'd settle down
But you are like a bramble-bush
That bounces all around

At times I couldn't forgive
Those things you did to me
And finally had to realize
Our love was not to be

You have to be who you are
I have no problem with that
You're doing the best you can
And I accept the fact

I can only wish you well
A journey free of strife
May the wind be at your back
Your dreams fullfilled in life

I could never hate you
No matter how hard I try
I can only love you
And never say, "goodbye"

Why You Are That Way?

Why you are that way
I will never know
Did you try to deny it?
Did it take root and grow?

I've tried to understand
That great change in your life
But the pain soon sweeps through me
Like a jagged twist of knife

No matter who you are
I will remain a friend
You'll always be special
If only I could pretend

Does it make a difference?
Of course, I'll always care
But I'm trying to grasp it all
As I'm plunged into despair

I drink, I smoke, I pray
I toss and turn all night
I write, I waunder through the day
But nothing makes it right

I can never look at you the same
And dream about what might have been
To love you in that "special way"
Is that such a sin?

To say it doesn't matter
Why live my life a lie
I'll accept you for who you are
And love you until I die

I Never Thanked You

You were my competitor
Other suitors passed through
But we hung on
All those years

Others tired of her games
Her heavy drinking
They used her
Or she used them

We saw beyond
Sweeping brunette strands
Wide dark eyes
Girlish laugh

We knew she was like
An unbroken horse
Spirited and untameable
Free as the wind

We saw her darkside
Too many times
Felt our hearts rip
When she hurt herself

We fiercely defended her
Always forgave her
Never stopped caring
Were there for her

We knew of her pain
Saw her fight back
Accomplish much
Never give up

We stayed in the race
To the final finish
Hoping to change her
Save her or something

Now, the race is over
We both lost
She's in another world
Neither of us understands

We're no longer competitors
We can't compete
Give her anything
Except our understanding

I never thanked you
You were good to her
And like me
You will love her always

IV. The Pain of Love

"A sickness full of woes, all remedies refusing."

-Samuel Daniel

I Think we Could Have Made it

I think we could have made it
Just how, I cannot say
But now the winds of change have come
And blown those dreams away

Mountains of Complexities
Doomed us from the start
Problems insurmountable
Kept us so apart

I know you loved me once
Saw it in your eyes
Felt it in your touch
Heard it in your sighs

The decency inside you
A fact you cannot hide
Believe it hurts you so
To know I'm breaking up inside

If fate was so against us
If it was never meant to be
At least I know inside of you
Remains a part of me

I think we could have made it
Why didn't we even try?
Took something that was beautiful
Turned it into a lie

It Would Have Been So Simple

It would have been so simple
Turn back the hand of time
Six or seven years ago
When you were a friend of mine

Now, when I'm around you
I always feel so tense
Wish I could lift the burden off
Give up the suspense

Casual conversation
Now, that would be great
Relaxed and not threatned
On a Platonic date

"How about those Packers?"
"After all these years?"
'Want to go for pizza?'
'Drink a couple beers?'

Watching you play softball
On a sultry summer's day
Stopping by to see you
Just to pass the time away

It would have been so simple
But I just can't pretend
When I fell in love with you
I lost you as my friend

"I Celebrate"

I celebrate your birthday
And wonder where you are
Probably doing the same as me
Sitting in some bar

But you are likely with some friends
Who give you toast and cheer
And I am sitting all alone
Nursing on a beer

I wanted this to be
A very special day
But I took the gifts I bought you
And gave them all away

We could have gone to dinner
Danced away the night
Closed our eyes, felt the warmth
Held each other tight

I wonder what your thinking now
We reflect on such a day
Hopes and dreams and those regrets
We have left along the way

The clock is striking twelve
I down another beer
Wishing I was with you
Instead of sitting here

I celebrate your birthday
Oh God, I miss you so
Feel the pain of loss
Creep down into my soul

The Things I Never Gave You

I thought about the presents
I gave you through the years
Closed my eyes and swallowed
And blocked a stream of tears

There were flowers in the spring
Violets blue and roses red
Heart-shaped boxes in the winter
That were tied with pretty thread

The cards that were delivered
For all the special days
That showed I wouldn't forget
And cared in many ways

There were lots of trinkets
Clothes and little charms
And darling little teddy-bears
You held within your arms

If you ever missed me
We never were apart
When you wore that necklace
Firmly against your heart

But I could never give you
What I wanted to most of all
The situation wouldn't allow it
So I stood behind a wall

A wall of pain and regret
It often drove me crazy
Knowing I could never give you
A diamond and a baby

Faded Pictures

I found the photo album
On a snow-filled winters night
The cloud of time soon cleared away
Pictures of the past soon shined bright

We looked so different then
So young and so care-free
I used to make you laugh
How you believed in me

How I once adored you
When you had that certain glow
We looked on with joy and wonder
As we watched the children grow

How I couldn't stay away from you
And missed you when we were apart
How did we lose those special feelings?
What magic died within the heart?

Dreams soon fade away
Like the last star before the dawn
We stand alone and bewildered
Wondering what went wrong

The house is empty now
No children's laughter to make it right
Just you and me alone together
With empty day and hollow night

Did it die slowly like a lilac bush
That yields less fruit throughout the years?
Leaving only the bloom of fragrance
Until that to dissappears?

I slowly turn the tattered pages
And through the mist of time I see
Faded pictures of the way it used to be
Faded pictures of you and me

I Wanted It All

I wanted it all
But I stayed away
Even though a moment without you
Appeared like a day

I stood in the shadows
Not taking a chance
Fearing rejection
Like the pierce of a lance

I wanted to love you
For the rest of my life
To be with you always
To make you my wife

I longed for a minature you
Dolled up in little dresses
The breeze catching her lace
The sun kissing her tresses

To grow old with you
On a warm summer's night
Just you and I on a porch swing
Holding you tight

Yes, I wanted it all
But I couldn't see
Time sift through my fingers
Like sand to the sea

I waited too long
The days turned to years
Opportunity died
And confirmed all my fears

Now, I'm old and alone
And I sit in a trance
Wishing only that
I had taken a chance

Enter Through The Doorway

Enter through the doorway
In a long white gown
Music starts to play
Families turn around

Your father gives you up
Proudly take your hand
Pledge my love eternal
With a golden band

Enter through the doorway
Feel a rush of joy
Climbs on to my lap
A bouncing baby boy

Enter through the doorway
With a skip and twirl
Shiny hair and outstreched arms
Its Daddy's little girl

The little house is radiant
Bathed in sunlight from above
Flowers bloom, the grass is green
A place of peace and love

A beautiful face before me
A smile thats warm and bright
But suddenly the color fades
To a grainy black and white

Everything is fading
Why, I do not know
All I ever wanted
Melts like April snow

The little house dissappears
Into a mist of gray
I reach out helplessly
But you to fade away

Reality rips through me
Hear the alarm clock's scream
Painfully aware it was
Nothing but a dream

You Flew To Me

Flew to me on velvet wings
A soft warm summer's night
Took my spirit made it soar
Turned darkness into light

Locked our hands together
Walked among the trees
Drew in the scent of forest
Caught the temperate breeze

Made music in a clearing
Rejoiced throughout the night
Counted all the stars
Held each other tight

Summers end too suddenly
Why, I'll never know
Passion dies so quickly
But leaves an ember glow

Your Cassandra's voice rang out
I refused to hear
Wanted you forever
Unwilling to face the fear

Wings of deceit lifted
You took off in flight
My heart a shattered pinata
A cold December's night

First loss, Last Loss

My puppy's name was Scruffy
He'd go everywhere I'd go
He'd meet me by the schoolbus
We'd frolick in the snow

Even as a child I knew
People can let you down
The only truth I knew
Was Scruffy was around

Scruffy would wait for me
Outside my best friend's home
One day I walked out and knew
That I was all alone

They found him lying peacefully
Beside an old oak tree
He must have stumbled up the road
To say goodbye to me

Mother tried to explain
Said,"Go ahead and cry"
"Just as everything must live
Everything must die"

"You're getting bigger now
Must accept the fact
We often lose the ones we love
And they never will come back"

Years have passed since that day
I've had my share of pain
Picked up the broken pieces
Marched right off again

Scruffy was my first loss
My last loss was you
Remember mother's words
Sometimes life is cruel

Maturity does not ease a loss
But I still must face the fact
You are gone like Scruffy
And Scruffy won't be back

The Last Regret

The last regret I have
Is how I walked away
Things were going nowhere
Knew I couldn't stay

Didn't leave a note
Didn't say goodbye
Didn't even call
Made you wonder,"why?"

Did I leave you puzzled?
Did you feel relief?
Do you feel resentful?
Are you filled with grief?

If I stayed around
I'd turn into a fool
Say something stupid
Like,"I want to marry you"

Thought I could make you happy
What a foolish goal!
Hoped I could change you
Reach into your soul

Finally had to realize
Things are not to be
But still regret, the way I left
The day I set you free

The Seashell

Love is like a special sea shell
It makes its own kind of music
Deep within the heart, the music plays
Like the sea shell, waiting for someone
To hear the music of peace
And comfort that comes from deep inside
Hear the shell, hear my heart
Lonely in love

What Ever Happened?

What ever happened to you?
Haven't seen you in years
Did your innocence die?
Mine did

Remember that summer
Light years ago?
A different time?
A different world?

There was polio
The Cold War raged
Some built bombshelters
But people believed in something

We'd take my baby sister
To the local grocery for icecream
I hear its a convenience store now
Everyone's in a hurry

At night, you would sneak over
We'd dance to Bobby Vinton records
On the back patio
Thought we knew about love

Didn't know much about sex
Only wanted to dance
Hold hands-enjoy the night
My kid brother would watch us

As we danced under starry skies
We were unaware of ominous clouds
Creeping up on America
Like a stauking wolf

What ever happened to you?
Did you stop believing?
I lost my faith in a jungle
And a divorce court

Did you lose your innocence?
I hope you didn't
The girl next door
My first love

V. The Lighter Side

Lovers- *"Unconscious comedians"*

When Will I Leave You?

There are so many songs about it
Like leaving in "The Twelth of Never"
Or never leaving in August
Or any kind of weather

So I wrote my own
To let you know
That I will never leave
In the sun, rain, or snow

You'll always keep me interested
I won't find you a bore
But if Tampa wins the Superbowl
I'll walk right out the door

If the Lions stay injury free
You'll see the last of me
If Lambeau Field doesn't sell out
I'll turn and run and flee

When players are paid what they're worth
And suceed in staying out of trouble
I'll run and pack my bags
And head out on the double

I'll hang in like a Cub-fan
You'll never see me leave
We're closer than a Packer-Lion game
I'll never give you the heave

Some Have A Puppy

When the customers get to them
And the boss is a jerk
Some have a puppy
To greet them from work

He patiently waits for them
All through the day
He yelps when he sees them
He's ready for play

Some have a kitten
To make them feel good
"I guess you can pet me"
Now, go get my food"

Some flee their problems
And head for the bar
Where no one's a loser
Everyone a star

Others find refuge
When their life is a mess
By turning to football
To relieve all the stress

Lions, and Packers, and Bears
Oh, my!
The Vikings and Cowboys
They'll whoop, shout, and cry

It starts in the Spring
And continues all year
They'll argue who's best
Then cry in their beer

The refuge for lazy
Is always TV
Mindless talk-shows
And NYPD

When life gets us down
When were saddest and blue
Some have a puppy
But I have you

You Snuck up on Me

My life was not really going well
But I was getting by
Loneliness was not much fun
But I could live the lie

Drifting by thoughtlessly
Giving romance a break
Met you, found drawn to you
That was my mistake

Tried to push my feelings back
"This can't happen to me?"
Complications multiplied
No longer felt so free

You snuck up and stole my heart
Like a thief in darkest night
Now, I find my life a mess
Can't seem to set things right

I was not expecting it
Caught me so off guard
Like a tornado to a trailer park
Hit me swift and hard

The Mid-Life Blues

The mid-life blues is killing me
I really should slow down
But find it quite impossible
When I have you around

Took you out the other night
The bouncer grinned at me
Must have thought, "You sly old dog"
When he asked for your ID

Took you to my home
Thought you such a tease
Eyed my record albums
Said, "What on earth are these?"

I think the Beatles were
The coolest group to hit this land
But when it comes to being awesome
Guns and Roses is your band

Thanksgiving with your family
I'd show up if I was able
Probably sit in the dinningroom
With you at some card table

I'm afraid I've pushed male menopause
A little bit too far
Perhaps I should give you up
And buy a small sportscar

Sweeter Than

I really have to admit
You are quite a find
Sweetest thing I've ever seen
Sweeter than cheap wine

Just to be around you
Is really quite a treat
You're sweeter than those lemon bars
That only Greeks must eat

Watching you standing there
Really drives me crazy
I really can't deny
You're more kissable than a baby

I hope your not offended
I hope it doesn't sound funny
But you are even cuter
Than a furry little bunny

If you ever say the word
I'd run off with you
Give up everything I had
Be a love-struck fool

Give up my wife and kids
If I had some kids and wife
To have a happy fling with you
The sugar of my life

Where Have They Gone?

Travelled to Wisconsin
Pulled into a little town
Streets and sidewalks empty
Where have the "Cheeseheads" gone?

No sign of life anywhere
Just vehicles parked by bars
Yards are left in disrepair
The mall is free of cars

Should I call Mulder and Scully
Maybe they would know
Has every single "cheesehead"
Been abducted by a UFO?

Does Wisconsin have a siesta
Where everything shuts down?
Or have they all migrated south
To escape this frozen town?

Pulled into a convience store
On the edge of town
Finally found someone and asked
"Where have the "cheeseheads" gone?"

"Listen, pal, don't get me wrong
But have you gone insane?
How dare you try to talk to me
During the Packer game?"

Should Have Seen

Should have seen the warning signs
Knew that you were trouble
Should have used my other head
Split out on the double

The bumper sticker on your car
Was more than just a clue
Should have caught the message
"Psycho's Have Rights Too"

If I understood your license plate
I wouldn't be in this fix
Only you would chose a plate that read
P.M.S. Six-Six-Six

Should have seen the warning signs
Even my dog knew
Turned Collie into Pit-Bull
When he first layed eyes on you

Should have seen the danger
Should have called retreat
Even non-Catholics crossed themselves
When we walked down the street

Everyone but me could see
I was a first-class clown
Wished I had read those warning signs
Before you brought me down

Didn't Make My Day

Old popcorn crunches beneath my shoes
Over-priced gooey candy between my teeth
I hold your hand
But your mind is elsewhere

There is not a dry eye
In the theater
But men and women often cry
For different reasons

"He loves her so much"
You must be thinking
But I love you even more
Gave up the Packer-Viking game for this

And babe, tonight better rock
Or you will never drag me
To another movie lacking both
Violence and women under thirty

The movie drags on
I wonder when Clint will
Dump her, blow up those bridges
Make my day

Love Can Be

Love can be sweet
As gobs of candy
But too much candy can lead
To a trip to the love-dentist

Sometimes, love is like
A cheap chocolate bunny
Delicious looking on the outside
Hollow on the inside

Love can be like icecream
Come in many flavors
Unfortunately, an unpopular favorite
Is rocky road

And like icecream
Love can lead to unpleasant surprises
A greedy gulp-ooch!
A surge of pain to the brain

Love can come to freely
Like cheap beer at a wedding
Guzzle it because its free
Pay the consequences later

Love if often like a box of chocolates
Usually don't get what you want
But isn't it fun squeezing
As many tastey morsels as possible?

VI. The Bitterness of Love

"Scratch a lover find a foe."

-Dorthy Parker

Have I Ever Thanked You?

Have I ever thanked you
For what you've done to me?
I finally snapped the chain of charm
And set my own self free

You finally crossed the line
And I'm never looking back
The burdens lifted off of me
My life is back on tract

Have I ever thanked you
For the swell of pain inside
Taking my heart and mind
For a roller-coaster ride?

When you're not around
You can never wrack my brain
Acting hot and cold
Driving me insane

Ping-ponging through life
As reckless as you dare
Knowing not who you are
But I no longer care

Thank you for the memories
I've learned my lessons well
I'd rather be without you
Then live inside your hell
Have I ever thanked you
For what you did to me?
Continue with your crazy games
But stay away from me

My Eve of Destruction

You are the "Eve"
Of my destruction
Lilith in the garden
A Pandora's box of trouble

You are Betty Davis
In her meanest role
Delilah with sizzors
Manipulative as Lady McBeth

A witch with the letter "B."
Shakespeare's shrew
Always find a way
To make someone a fool

You are all
Men hate and fear
Emasculating and castrating
Neurotic when not psychotic

"What goes around comes around"
That sayings really true
So you better watch out
Or someone might drop a house on you

The Showdown

Trying to avoid you
In this "one horse town"
It was really quite impossible
That I wouldn't see you around

Part of me wanted to see you
But I soon remembered the pain
Knew you were not good for me
Felt my emotions drain

It was so likely
When I ran into you
I would have my guard down
Stand there like a fool

Walking toward each other
We put our heads down
Then look up and confront
A "Wild West Showdown"

Should I make the first move?
Or let you draw first?
One false move, I believe
Can bring on all the worst

Painful memories flood back
All these dreadful nights
All the things you did to me
All those bitter fights

You turn on a phony smile
Look at me with surprise
I draw first and shoot
Rake you with machine-gun eyes

Threw Me For A Loss

Threw me for a loss
Before the whistle blew
Charged right through the line
Said that we were through

I was not expecting it
The cheap shot put on me
"A Martin-MacMahon like hit"
Left me lying helplessly

Wind knocked out of me
Spread-eagled on the ground
But mark my words
I'll be back, you won't keep me down

Like a phoenix from its ashes
I'll rise up to attack
Like the Packers of the Nineties
You'll see me spring right back

Success is the best revenge
Just you wait and see
The day will come and you'll regret
How you walked out on me

Should I Compare

Should I compare thee to a winter's day?
Thou art more bitter and cold
Rough winds do rip through us
And winter's lease is way too long
Sometimes too cold the heavens darken
And often is as gloomey as your complextion
If fair declines, you have slid fast
Not by chance, but by choice, the wrong choice
But thy miserable winter won't fade
Nor lose possession of your iciness
Only death can brag our miserable end
When eternal lines wear you down
So long as I breathe or see
So long lives this, that you have given pain to me

We Can Be Friends

"We can be friends"
Or so you say
Forget the past
Push the hurt away

Got over me quickly
Everything's just fine
Conveniently shelve the memories
Shove the past behind

We shared so much together
Had such intimacy
Now, we walk seperate paths
Because you chose to flee

Told each other secrets
Shared each hidden fear
Believed you loved me
Thought you were sincere

Act as if nothing happened
It didn't mean a thing!
We had something special
Not a short-lived fling !

Now, you have "the eggs"
To say it didn't mean a lot
Sure, we can be friends
As teenagers say,"Not!"

You Annoy Me

There was a time
When I enjoyed your company
But not anymore
You annoy me

More than those cards
That fall out of magazines
More than a certain
Hyper TV fitness star named Richard

You're as tasteful
As a plain bagel
About as sharp
As kindergarten sizzors

I'd rather watch TV reruns
See if "my little buddy"
Makes it off the island
Then spend another moment with you

Maybe I should do something
Less painful than be around you
Perhaps, I should call my dentist
Make an appointment

VII. Love and Marriage

Marriage- *"The dawn of marriage, and marraage is the sunset of love."*
-Anon.

When You Had That Glow

When you had that glow
Fullfilled a childhood dream
Skin gave off a radiance
Eyes a happy gleam

The most special bond
Between a husband and a wife
Blissful expectation
The precious gift of life

Standing there so beautiful
Proudly smile at me
Take my hand in yours
Squeeze it eagerly

Will it be a girl?
Will it be a boy?
Does it really matter
When both will bring us joy?

Pull you close and kiss you
Feel a tiny kick of life
Love you and adore you
Mother, Friend, and wife

Grandma Rocking

The rocking chair squeaks
The only sound in the night
You touch his little cheeks
His tiny fist clutched tight

Kneel by the rocker
My head against your shoulder
Close my eyes-pretend
Were not getting older

Remember days long ago
You rocked our baby boys
Memories and special moments
All the hopes and joys

Open eyes and smile
You grin back at me
Baby closes eyes
Sleeps so peacefully

Love my baby grandson
That precious little jewel
Love his father and uncle
And his grandma too

The Changing Sea

Satin sheets
Satin skin
Lightning hands
Searching tongues

The sweet smell of ocean
The sea troughs
Then crests
Builds to gale force

Breakers against rocks
Hair flies
Shadows dance
Sea boils

You scream
I explode
We collapse
Bathed in saltwater

Tide recedes
Cup your neck
Kiss happy tears
A tranquil sea

What Do You See?

What do you see
Gazing in the mirror?
Still pluck every gray hair?
Count every wrinkle?

What do you think
When you catch me
Checking out pretty young girls
In short dresses and jeans?

Do you remember when
I couldn't keep my hands away?
Kissed you, held you
Constantly made love to you?

Now, I bury myself
In a newspaper or book
Or glue my eyes
To the television screen

Do you reflect on times
When young men raced to wait on you?
Asked you to dance?
Turned and admired your beauty?

Do you view time
A raging river
Overspilling its banks
Eroding your youth?

Do you view age
Time's evil conspirator
An invincible enemy
That will defeat you in the end?

Do you see your mother's hands
Looking back through soapy dishwater?
I see someone who has defeated time and age
The woman, I chose to love forever

Drifts

Outside the wind rages
Snow pellets the windows
Furnace kicks in again
Wrap the comforter around me

The snow is as white
As your skin
But unlike you
Cold to the touch

Snow drifts, I drift
A certain Spring night
Wipers swish slowly
Gentle perfumed rain

Soft music plays
Windows down
A steady temperate breeze
Teases your hair

Suddenly an updraft
Catches your white dress
I try not to look
Catch my breath

Ivory legs revealed
You blush
But must have felt like Marilyn
In that movie

For a moment
You are a goddess
Worthy of my
Adoration

Snow drifts, mind drifts
A Spring goddess
You as white
As the swirling snow

Flowers In The Night

Certain flowers sometimes give
A different scent at night
And you, my love
Are like such flowers

Emerge from the bathroom
Perfumed hair down
Chestnut eyes glow
In anticipation

Stand proudly before me
Ribbons of light in your hair
Loosen robe
Shoulders shimmer

I watch in awe
Robe slides to the floor
Approach the banquet
Flowers in the night

What Is Their Secret?

Saw them walking toward me
An old couple holding hands
Asked myself
"What is their secret?"

Sometimes, I'm so cynical
Think long-loving relationships
Are about as common
As mirrors at a Jewish funeral

Why did they stay together?
Was their generation stronger?
Or were they swept up in
The simplicity of their formative years?

Back then, social and economic pressures
Probably forced people to make it work
They put up with more
Forgave a lot

Today, we have so many choices
I often wonder if we
Know what we want
Or who we really are

The old couple approaches
The woman-hunched over-lined face
The man-whisp of white hair
Paunch-pants above the waist

He holds her withered hand proudly
As if she were a pretty model
She gives an admiring glance
As if he were a handsome prince

They smile and greet me
I realize they love each other
I walk by and hesistate
Then continue my journey

Will you hold my hand
Twenty-five years from now?
I regret, I didn't go back
Ask them,"What is your secret?"

Index of First Lines

Beware of toxic people 15
Blues music blares 33

Catch your gaze 42
Certain flowers give 103

Do you know that woman? 16

Enter through the doorway 64

Football seasons come at last 41
Found an old dusty lamp 6
Flew to me on velvet wings 66

Games of the mind 13

Has life dealt you cruelly? 17
Have I ever thanked you? 87
Have you heard the fable? 20
Hitler built the autobaun 38

I celebrate your birthday 58
I could never hate you 49
I do the same as I did then 27
I'd rather be lonely 9
I found the photo album 60
If you don't watch out 36
If you ever asked me to 11
I love horses 19
I really have to admit 80
I really think we could have made it 56
I thought about the presents 59
I wanted it all 62
It would have been so simple 57

Love can be sweet	84
Love is like a special seashell	70
Love is not a faucet	3
Maybe it sounds funny	35
Met you in highschool	18
My puppy's name was Scruffy	67
My life was not really going well	78
Old popcorn crunches beneath my shoes	83
Outside the wind rages	101
Satin sheets	98
Saw them walking toward me	104
Searching for your inner-self	37
Should I compare thee to a winter's day	91
Sometimes we have to use our head	12
The dream became a nightmare	31
The highway of love	22
The last regret I have	69
The lighter side of you	30
The mid-life blues is killing me	79
The New Year has come at last	39
The path you chose to take	28
The rocking chair squeeks	97
The solution may sound crazy	14
There are so many songs about it	75
There's an old sea story	45
There was a time	93
There was a pretty young maid	20
Threw me for a loss	90
Travelled to Wisconsin	81
Trying to avoid you	89

You are the "Eve"	88
You're strong and proud	46
We can be friends	92
We filled a void together	5
What are you afraid of?	8
What do you see?	99
What ever happened to you?	71
When you had that glow	97
When the customers get to them	76
With a cheetah's speed you race	34
Why do I draw them?	44
Why you are that way?	51
You stand there so smugly	4
You were my competitor	52

Return to the Diner

Charlie started to slip, but regained his balance by grabbing the side mirror of the taxi.

"Going home, Charlie?," Tom asked.

"You got her, sure is cold out."

"Minnesota got hit bad."

"They always get hit hard," Charlie began, "Difference between Minnesota and Wisconsin is, Minnesota is one degree colder, and has one more Norwegian. I should know, I lived there and counted them."

"You've been just about everywhere."

"Drunks more around a lot." The taxi pulled up to a rundown house.

"Charlie, when are you going to shovel your sidewalk?"

"Never, it'll melt in a few months."

"Doesn't the city get after you?"

"They gave up on me like everyone else."

"Why are you so hard on yourself?"

"I should be. Don't have any friends." Charlie paused,

"Had friends but they beat me up the other night....snuck up on me."

"Do I know them?"

"Yeah, Jim Beam and Jack Daniels," Charlie hit Tom lightly on the shoulder, "Got ya."

Charlie's smile faded. He turned toward Tom. "Tom, you always took care of me and I never thanked you. I used to think you were too smart for this, but you're smart and you're the best."

"Why, thanks Charlie," Tom said with surprise. "See you later."

"See you later," Charlie said with a laugh. He shut the taxi door and staggered up the steps. Charlie pushed his door open. He never bothered to lock it. "The pictures," he mumbled as he nearly fell over his couch. He regained his balance, turned on a light, kicked an empty beer can, and entered the small kitchen. There wasn't much whiskey left, but it would do. He coughed at first, but his throat soon felt warm. It would give him the strenghth to do it, but first he would have to call his sister, and explain. He found her phone number beneath an overflowing ashtray. The whiskey went down better the second time, he fumbled for his matches, lit a cigarette, stared at the scrap of paper and started to loosen his belt.

Cathy regretted she didn't call the restaurant to see if she was needed. The wind howled and her car rocked, as she drove over the icy bridge. The windshield wipers made a snapping sound, as they started to ice up. 'I can't take much more of this,' she thought. The diner's light was barely visible in the swirling snow. Her heart was still pounding when she entered the Diner.

Ralph the cook, and Nancy, the other waitress were sitting at the counter talking quietly.

"So when are you going to get out of that crazy relationship," she heard Ralph say. Nancy shrugged and bowed her head.

Nancy was wearing sunglasses, and Cathy reasoned her boyfriend hit her again.

"Hi, guys," Cathy announced. Ralph turned toward her.

"I should have called you," Ralph began, "It's been really dead, but you're here, so what the hell."

"You'd have to be crazy," Cathy commented, "To go out in this weather."

"So that means we'll get a few people," Ralph said with a grin.

David and Michelle sat across from each other in their favorite booth in the back of the bar. David took a swallow of his beer and Michelle tipped her glass and guzzled. "Well," she began, "I'm ready for another. How about you?"

"Not yet," David replied in an even voice, "Do you have to drink so fast?"

"I always drink fast," Michelle replied, as she stood up. David watched her head for the bar and shook his head. When she returned, he could already see a wild, glassy look in her eyes.

"Too bad they don't have tap beer," Michelle commented. "We could drink more for less."

"I want to enjoy my beer, not slam them like you."

"Take away the tap beer and turn the music down and keep out the riff-raff, right, David?"

"If you say so."

"I know bars, I grew up in them. A bar gets the clientele it wants," Michelle said in a hurried voice. "Drink up, I'm buying." She tipped her glass and took another swallow. Her eyelashes started to quiver.

"Do you know why you like this place?"

David shruggged. "It makes you feel like an intellectual. When I first moved here and saw all these bars, I thought, Wow!" Michelle let out a giggle. "It was almost like a religious experience. This is the place!" She reached over and tapped David on the shoulder. "This city is to a drunk what Vegas is to a gambler. Don't like the bar you're in, walk ten feet. Right, Dave?"

"Whatever you say," David replied.

"I just noticed something," Michelle said, as she stood up, "The Packers won the Super Bowl, but you wouldn't know it looking around here."

"I think the word is out about the Packers."

"They don't have pennants on the walls," she said as she tipped her glass. "They have paintings without beer signs. What a weird place."

Michelle set her glass down and pointed to a painting of a semi-clad woman with long red hair. Her head was resting on a knee. "Do you think she's beautiful?"

"Yes," David replied, "But its only a painting."

"Only a painting," Michelle said in an excited voice."Do you think there's a story behind it? Like he really loved her and wanted to make her immortal? Or maybe he just needed the money, or he loved her and needed money."

"Michelle, sit down!"

She slumped into the booth and started to run her fingers through her hair. "Brunnettes are three things-pretty, average, or ugly. Do you know what redheads are? They are either gorgeous or anemic-looking. Don't you agree?"

"I never really thought about it," David answered, "I guess I like all kinds."

"David," Michelle said as she continued to pull on her hair. "I think I'm going to dye my hair red. Would you like me with red hair?"

"You'd look anemic," he answered quietly.

"Oh, the funny guy is back," she said as she downed the last of her beer. Michelle's eyes widened. "Do you know what I am?"

"What kind of question is that?"

"I'm a twenty-nine year old alcoholic."

"Oh, gee, and we promised not to keep secrets from each other."

"Look at me funny man," her voice became harsh. She pointed below her eyes. "These are crows feet and the rest of me is starting to sag. I'm hitting the big three-0 in a few months."

"You make it sound like thirty is almost dead."

"It is if you're a woman. You know age and beauty and when that's gone, you're nothing unless you have money. I'll become a throwaway in our "can't use it anymore society."

"I'd never throw you away."

"Oh, really," she said as she slammed her drink down hard. The bartender and a few patrons turned. David grabbed her arm and said in a hushed voice, "Everyone is looking at us, so mellow out."

"Anything you say," Michelle said calmly. "You said that pot makes me mellow. Want to burn one?" She opened her purse, but David reached over snapped her purse and yanked it toward him. "Are you nuts?"

"Are you going to hit me? Why don't you hit me? Is it because you're so noble?"

"I wasn't brought up that way. Men don't hit women no matter what they do."

"But sometimes its good for them. It erases some of the guilt like when your little and naughty and get spanked, everything evens out, but if you don't get spanked, you feel worse."

"Why do you have to talk so sick at times?"

"I'm a bad little girl," she purred, "I need a spanking." A huge grin appeared on her face and without warning she yelled, "Spank me!"

David covered his eyes, "I guess we won't be comming in here for awhile."

"Wow," Michelle continued in her little girl voice, "Did you see everyone look? Boy, do you look mad. I thought you liked the little girl in me."

"The little girl, yes, not the bratty little kid," David replied. He still had his eyes covered.

"Did you know alcoholics are the biggest liars in the world? she began, "We should all go into politics. I could say I'm sorry for embarassing you and I could say it like I really meant it. We drunks are so good at acting sincere, we're always sorry." She lifted her hands and wiggled her fingers. "We are always on the verge of getting it together, but you know what? We don't care what we do or who we hurt. We only care about that next drink, and guess what, I could use another drink."

"Don't you think you've had enough?"

"Oh, I haven't heard that before." Michelle smiled, "Have you ever heard of Tex Ritter?"

"Of course, he was a singing cowboy."

"A singing cowboy with a white hat," Michelle added, "only the good guys wore white hats and got to sing. It must have been so simple back then. Daddy-drunkest had his music on the bar's jukebox. He'd play this song,"Hillbilly Heaven" over and over. Tex would sing about all these dead country singers up in heaven and you know what?"

"I don't even want to guess."

"I made up a song about the Diner. Want to hear it. Its called "Loser Heaven."

"You're going to sing aren't you?," David covered his face.

"Don't worry, I'll keep it real soft."

> I dreamed I was there in loser heaven
> And all the Diner people were there
> There's Charlie, the Viet Nam drunk
> That old lady that smells like a skunk
> And Nancy, whose boyfriend treats her bad
> Isn't that sad?
> There's David and Michelle as well
> They live in their private hell

Her voice trailed off. "So how do you like it?" "Don't quit your day job."

"I think I need a beer. One more and I should be able to drink myself sober. I don't want any of that "American slop," as you call it. Get me something fancy."

"Okay," David said as he got up slowly. Michelle grabbed his arm and said, "Get me something out of that grab bag thing. I like surprises."

David walked wearily up to the bar. The brunette bartender forced a smile. "Two grabs." He ran his fingers through the plastic bowl and pulled out two pieces of paper. "One for me and one for "psychobrat." The bartender grinned and whispered, "How do you stand it?"

"You can't chose who you care about, but it does make life interesting." The bartender nodded in agreement.

"You like brunettes best," Michelle said with a smile. "I saw you check her out."

"She's just nice, that's all. Besides she's too young for me."

"Is the cradle-robber getting morals," Michelle inquired, as she lifted her bottle? "Sip don't slam, right Darling?" David nodded.

"I know a lot about science," she said suddenly, "Everything kills or uses something in order to survive. Don't you agree?"

"Have you ever considered joining an optimist club?"

"You see, Darling, its so simple." She pointed to the painting. "She got used, the artist got used, everyone in this bar gets used and so does everyone at the Diner, and David, we use each other. You put up with me and act calm and use wit and sarcasm to get back at me, but I can handle that. You use me to make you feel young again. I'm your midlife crisis trophy chick. And you don't really love me."

"Of course I love you," David said, as he turned away." I put up with you don't I?"

"Oh, the noble martyr. Mister, my wife doesn't understand me. Oh, I'm so impressed." She let out a cackle.

"I'm tired of playing scientist," Michelle said evenly. "I want to play psychologist..I came from a dysfunctional family. She lifted her beer. "A toast to dysfunctional, the most overused word of the 1990's. We always become what we hate. When I was little, I used to drag my drunken mother into the house. I hated her, and my father, who just took off, well I hated him too. And guess what? I've become them. You know the big difference between your drinking and mine? You drink to dull the pain and I drink to obliterate it, but guess what? The pain comes back." She stood up and lifted the beer bottle,'Time to obliterate, Cheers." She emptied the bottle in one big gulp. "I think I'm sober again. Lets go to the Diner. I'm sorry I was such a bitch."

David took her hand and they walked out the door. A rush of wind caught Michelle's hair blowing it into her eyes.

"Cool," Michelle said with a laugh. She fell against the car door.

"Get in," David said briskly, "Its freezing out." Michelle slumped into the car. David started the car and backed it out. Michelle slid against his shoulder. David turned to her. "Sit up and pretend you're an adult, I can barely see in this crap!" She sat up, turned away, and silently stared out the window.

"My hands are cold," Michelle whined, as the got out of the car.

David squeezed her hands, "Why don't you wear gloves?"

"I always lose them."

"Maybe you should get mittens and tie them to your sleeve like a little kid." She let go of his hands and charged toward the restaurant door.

By the time David entered the restaurant, Michelle was already sitting in the back booth. He wearily approached and sat down across from her.

"Just coffee," David said, as Cathy approached.

"Are you mad at your little Michelle," She teased?

"I could never stay mad at you."

"Do you think I'm your sub-conscious daughter?"

"Still on the psychology kick?"

"You treat me like a little girl at times. We go to the park in the summer and stuff."

"Am I your substitute father?"

"David, sometimes your so paternal. What is the first thing you would do if I was your daughter?"

"Ground you and you know what you would do?"

"Sneak out a window," thay said in unison. They laughed and clicked their coffee cups together.

"David," her tone became serious, "remember when you asked me if I wanted to be a mother?"

"Yes," David replied softly.

"You said the last time you wanted someone to have your baby, I was a baby. I laughed, but it really hurt."

"Why is that?," He reached over and took both her hands.

"Because I don't want to be a mother. All girls do in a way, but its too late for me." She squeezed his hands and repeated, "Too late."

"The age thing again, you've got plenty of time."

"Its not a matter of age." Her voice became weak. "A baby wouldn't settle me, it would only slow me down. Michelle is stuck on fast-forward."

Cathy returned and refilled their coffee cups. Michelle watched her walk away. She turned to David. "Do you know who the smartest people in the world are? They don't have fancy degrees or high IQ's. Give up?"

David shrugged.

"Waitresses," she replied with a smile," and bartenders, cab drivers, and perhaps, cops. you want to know why?"

"The suspense is killing me."

"Because they know people. In a few minutes they know what your game is."

"I guess that makes sense in a Michelle sort of way."

Cathy returned to the booth. "Do you guys want anything? I'm going on break."

"I think we're fine," David answered. Michelle shook her head and grinned.

"Something I should know about?," David inquired.

"She thinks your handsome. What do you think of that?"

"If they're not the smartest people in the world, they at-least have good eyesight," David replied with a smile.

"Good, I'm glad I got you smiling. Cathy also said you have the softest blue eyes she's ever seen"

"Is that so," David said with a blush.

"When I go into bitch-mode, you always look away from me," Michelle stated. "Why is that?"

"Can you blame me?"

"You should have looked at me at the bar, because eyes don't tell lies."

"What are you talking about?"

"The eyes always tell the truth. You see, David, I know you love me. I see the way you look at me at times. How many people love David? Your sons? Perhaps your wife? I wouldn't be surprised if Cathy loved you. Lots of people love you."

She lifted her middle finger and asked, "Do you know what this means?"

"Of course."

"It has two meanings actually." Michelle smiled weakly. "Up yours and how many people love Michelle."

"Oh, Michelle," David whispered, as he put his head down.

"Since Michelle hates Michelle," she said in a steady voice. "I wonder who the mystery masochist is? Cathy told me once, Michelle, David sees something special in you." A tear rolled down her cheek. "Your Michelle is special."

David reached over and took her hands, "You will always be my special Michelle," he whispered, "Always."

"David," she asked as she looked up at him. "Why can't you cry? You're more Alan Alda than John Wayne, so why can't you cry? You cry for me inside every night, don't you?"

David turned away and swallowed. "If you can't cry for you, then cry for us, because there is no us, its over, David. I don't want to see you anymore. If you really love me, you will stay away. We're killing each other and I want to kill myself by myself."

"Would you look at that," Ralph said as he tapped Cathy's shoulder. "This place is getting weirder all the time." Both Cathy and Nancy turned. Michelle was cradling David and he was sobbing.

"What are you looking at," Michelle screamed, "Were not freaks, you're the freaks!" Ralph, Cathy, and Nancy turned away at the same time.

The door of the Diner swung open and a middle-aged woman entered. "I hope thats not David's old lady," Ralph whispered. "Its not," Nancy said, "She's much younger."

"So this is the famous Diner," the woman said as she looked around. "Which one of you is Cathy?" Cathy raised her hand. "And you must be Nancy?" Nancy nodded.

Michelle timidly approached the cash registerer "I want to apoligize," she stammered, "It's just that David, I think you're great people."

"Thats okay, Michelle," Cathy said softly, "We often say things we don't mean."

"So you're little Michelle," the woman interupted, "and that man back there must be David."

"Who in the hell are you?," Ralph barked.

"Why, you must be Ralph, Charlie really liked you. You reminded him of his Sergeant. He said you were a teddy bear with an attitude. I'm Charlie's sister, Margaret I just drove in from Janesville."

"How's Charlie?," Ralph inquired with a grin.

"That's why I'm here," she replied in a weak voice, "Charlie's dead."

"But he can't be," Cathy whispered, "he sits over there."

"I'm afraid so," Margaret continued, "I need to sit down." She slumped into a stool.

"Poor old Charlie," Nancy said as she bowed her head.

"In a way it was for the best," Margaret said softly, "he was in a lot of pain. The real Charlie died a long time ago."

"How?," Ralph asked.

"He killed himself," Margaret replied. She turned to Nancy, "Could I have a glass of water?" Nancy handed her a glass. She took a swallow. "Could I ask you all a favor? Her voice trembled. "Would you come to his funeral? Its on Tuesday I don't want to be the only one there."

"Of course we'll come," Ralph said softly.

"Did you know that this was his home and you were his family?," Margaret stated.

The Diner's door swung open again and Tom, the taxi driver, entered. "Did you hear about Viet Nam Charlie? He's dead, I just can't believe it."

"We just found out," Ralph said. "This is Charlie's sister." Margaret turned and nodded.

"Maybe we should have a moment of silence," Tom suggested.

"Girls, would you help me up?," Margaret asked. Cathy and Nancy both took a hand. They formed a circle in front of the counter. Outside the wind picked up.

"I'm ready to sit down," Margaret said finally. She took another gulp of water. "It was never easy for Charles. We came from what they now call a dysfunctional family. I don't know what they called it then. When trouble started, he would always get me out of the house. I was the baby sister and he was so protective of me. When he went to Viet Nam, I felt like he betrayed me. I was only ten and you know when you're a child, you just don't understand things. When he came back." she let out a sob, "He changed." She pulled out a tissue and blew her nose. "Do you know how he got his nickname?"

"Well," Ralph replied, "I suppose his name was Charlie and he went to Viet Nam."

"Not really," Margaret explained. "Over there the enemy was nicknamed "Charlie". One day Charlie said, "I'm Charlie, I'm everyone's enemy." Then he laughed like a maniac and said, "I'm Viet Nam Charlie."

Everyone tried to help him. He stayed with me for awhile, but I just couldn't take it. He didn't get violent, he just got drunk and didn't make any sense. He came back a few times, but finally drifted up here. I hadn't seen him in two years."

She turned toward Cathy and Nancy, "Do you know someone named Grace?"

"Oh, sure," Nancy replied, "she's a sweet old lady that comes in here."

"You see," Margaret began slowly, "He called me the other night and said Princess. He hadn't called me that in years. Charles was back for a moment." She wiped a tear from her face. "Princess, I can't take it anymore, because of Grace's pictures. He hung up and then he must have done it. Does anyone know what he meant by Grace's pictures?"

"Sure," Cathy announced, "They were pictures of her grandaughter.

"Oh my God, that explains it," Margaret moaned. "One night Charles got drunker than usual and he told me something." She held her breath for a few seconds. "When he was over there." She took a quick breath. "A little girl came running toward him, it reminded him of the way I used to run to him when I got off the schoolbus, but then he remembered where he was and this girl was carrying something." She looked around, "She was carrying a grenade. Charles said you did things automatically over there. You thought about it afterwards. He laughed crazy and said, "automatic, my gun was on automatic." She grabbed Nancy's hand. Her voice became shrill, "He cut her in half, cut her in half." After a long pause, she downed the last of her water. "He said I killed three people that day-I killed her, I killed me, and I killed you, Princess." Margaret buried her head in her hands.

Margaret finally composed herself and stood, "I'll be okay, I'm staying at the motel down the road. I'll stop in for lunch," she smiled thinly.

"Tom, I need a taxi," Michelle said.

"Well, sure....okay."

"What a night," Ralph said as he shook his head, "I feel like drinking again."

"Don't you ever say that," Nancy said firmly.
"Have I ever told you about my lousy life?"

"About a zillion times."

"I work at this crumby place, watch TV and if that doesn't put me to sleep, I listen to my boring tapes. Besides if I drink, I could get women."

"How's that?"

"You see," Ralph pointed to his head, "The brain cells are coming back. Women want a guy who has everything or nothing. Everything makes a lot of sense; they have security and material things to flaunt, so they can brag. If they can't have eveything they chose a guy with nothing, a drunk or somebody that doesn't want to work or something like that. They get sympathy and attention. They feel needed, and they have the game and challenge of trying to change him. If women can't brag, they want to complain. You women like to bitch."

"I didn't think you thought women were so shallow"

"Oh, but men are shallow too, we don't come from Mars or Venus, we come from a planet even further away. A place where there is little oxygen."

"Are you sure you haven't fallen off the wagon already? How about a ride home?"

"If you promise not to talk about your jerk boyfriend"

"We're through"

"Yeah, right"

Nancy followed Ralph to the door and turned, "Teddy bear with an attitude, I like that."

"Stick with Sergeant Snorkel," Ralph said gruffly, "It's shorter."

David stepped out of the restroom as he wiped water off his face. "Sorry about the scene earlier."

"No problem. I thought it would have happened a long time ago, but you know it's for the best."

"Yes, Cathy, but she's..."

"I know David, she will always be special to you."

"Michelle said everyone at the Diner is a loser."

"Michelle says a lot of things when she's drunk. Want some coffee?" David shook his head. "Funny how people come and go in your life. I didn't even know Charlie had a sister."

"But he always returned to the Diner," David said quietly.

"Yes, he always returned to the Diner." Cathy said as she poured a cup of coffee. "I have to do something." She carried the cup over to the table. It rattled in the saucer. "Here you go, Charlie, enjoy."

"I already had one woman get weird on me tonight. Is there some sort of female virus going around?"

"David, sometimes we have to do weird things in order to keep from getting weird. You know, like when people whisper when they want to scream?" David nodded. "David, I think we both need a hug." They held each other for a long time, their hands clutched tightly. Finally Cathy stepped back, but continued to hold his hands. Sheets of snow lashed the windows.

"David, we're not losers, were survivors and I know the difference because I'm a waitress."

A Candid Interview

Editor: "Where do you get your ideas?"

Dennis Gibbons: "Sometimes an idea just pops into my head and at other times I reflect and then write."

ED: "Could you give a few examples?"

D.G.: "One time I was watching a cheetah on TV and I thought about the rat race. The result was my poem, "The Race." Another time I was watching my neices and nephews trying to hit a pinata and I thought of a broken heart being like a shattered pinata. Then I wrote,"You Flew To Me."

ED: "You mentioned reflecting"

D.G.: My brother, Terry, asked me about a girl from high school. He used to watch us dance on the back patio and wondered what ever happened to her. I thought about youth and innocence and proceeded to write, "What Ever Happened To You?"

ED: "That particular poem brings up the Viet Nam theme. Are you still trying to deal with it?"

D.G.: "In a way, yes. I didn't go through anything near what some people did over there. For awhile, it was almost vogue to be a Viet Nam vet. It shadows me, but doesn't stauk me."

ED: "Is Viet Nam Charlie based on a real person?"

D.G.: "Unfortunately, yes

ED: "You write a variety of love poems. Are they all you?"

D.G.: "I'm a sentimental slob and a cynical jerk. My mood fits my writing.'

ED: "Do you write about the same girl over and over?"

D.G.: "You're not the first person to ask me that. Some women in my writing are based on actual people, some are composites, and some sheer imagination."
I know I should sprinkle my writing with more blondes and redheads."

ED: "You do appear to prefer brunettes"

D.G.: It does appear that way but like David in, "<u>Return To The Diner,</u>" I like all kinds."

ED: "Do you believe in the perfect woman?"

D.G. "Of course not. Women are human just like men. I have to enjoy being around a woman and I don't want her to drive me crazy."

ED: "Have any driven you crazy?"

D.G.: "Is this a trick question?"

ED: "Lets turn to alcohol. You write about it a lot. Why?

D.G.: "I could answer that my jobs revolve around it, but the main reason is I've seen so many people ruin their lives with it."

ED: "Do you drink?"

D.G.: "I'm a writer."

ED: "Do you consider your self a social critic?"

D.G.: "I'm more a social observer. I'm not on a soapbox. My life is far from perfect. How dare I judge others?"

ED: "You mention the Green Bay Packers in your writing. Why are you wearing a Detroit Lions jacket?"

D.G.: "I was born in Detroit and they have the neatest uniforms."

ED: "What are your plans for the future?"

D.G.: "I still have a poem or two inside me. I work hard and play hard and know I should settle down."

ED: "Will you?"

D.G.: "Sure, as soon as I find the perfect woman."

About The Author

Dennis Gibbons was born in Detroit, Michigan. He has lived in Florida, California, and Minnesota, but has spent most of his life in Wisconsin. Gibbons graduated from The University of WI-La Crosse with majors in History, Broad Field Social Studies, and English. During the Viet Nam War, he worked with Operations Intellegence aboard the crusier, St. Paul.

Gibbons is the author of two other books. Sun and Rain is a collection of poetry and prose reflecting the Viet Nam era. Thinking of You is a collection of romantic poetry. He is currently living in Wisconsin and busy working on his next book.

Order Form:

COMPLETE & MAIL TO:

Mail Order Fulfillment
Words & Phrases
2231 South 14th Street
La Crosse, Wisconsin 54601

_____ copies of "The Light and the Dark" @ $12.50 ea. _____

_____ copies of "Thinking of You" @ $11.50 ea. _____

_____ copies of "Sun & Rain" @ $10.95 ea. _____

Total order _____

PUBLISHER PAYS SHIPPING:

Make check or money order out to author